Desert Critter Friends

Smelly Tales

Mona Gansberg Hodgson
Illustrated by Chris Sharp

CPH
SAINT LOUIS

*Many thanks to my editors at Concordia,
Dawn Weinstock and Ruth Geisler.*

*Special thanks to Charles and Freda for sharing
the ocean view from their living room with me.*

Desert Critter Friends Series

Friendly Differences

Thorny Treasures

Sour Snacks

Smelly Tales

Scripture quotations taken from the HOLY BIBLE, NEW INTERNATIONAL VERSION®. NIV®. Copyright © 1973, 1978, 1984 by International Bible Society. Used by permission of Zondervan Publishing House. All rights reserved.

Copyright © 1998 Mona Gansberg Hodgson

Published by Concordia Publishing House
3558 S. Jefferson Avenue, St. Louis, MO 63118-3968
Manufactured in the United States of America

Library of Congress Cataloging-in-Publication Data

Hodgson, Mona Gansberg, 1954–
    Smelly tales / Mona Gansberg Hodgson : illustrated by Chris Sharp.
        p.   cm. — (Desert critter friends ; bk 4)
    Summary: Rosie the skunk and her desert animal friends learn that gossip hurts and that a way of sharing God's love is to be truthful and to not tell tales.
    ISBN 0-570-05071-5
    [1. Skunks—Fiction. 2. Desert animals—Fiction. 3. Gossip—Fiction. 4. Friendship—Fiction. I. Sharp, Chris, 1954-   ill. II. Title. III. Series.
PZ7.H6649Sm   1998
[E]—dc21   97-48706
                                                  AC

1 2 3 4 5 6 7 8 9 10   07 06 05 04 03 02 01 00 99 98

Rosie, the striped skunk, tied
her tennis shoes before stepping
outside.

As Rosie walked down the path, she said hello to a red cardinal. Next she waved at a blue butterfly. Then Rosie turned onto the path that led to Bert's bush house. This was her day to go exploring with the roadrunner.

Suddenly Rosie heard a voice. She stopped to listen. Taylor, the tortoise, was reading something about friends.

Rosie stepped up behind Taylor. "I like poetry," she said. *Achoo!*

Taylor sniffed. After ducking his head into his shell, he pulled his book up against the opening.

Rosie stared at Taylor. Then she scratched her head.

The tortoise cleared his throat. Then he spoke in a muffled voice. "Uh … Rosie," he began. He took three steps backward. "I didn't expect to see you here." He backed up a couple more steps. "Uh … I was working on my speech for the opening of the new clubhouse."

"Bert and I are going to look for the best place to build it," Rosie said. "Do you want to come along?"

"No. Uh ..." The tortoise backed up some more, holding his book in front of his face. "I'd better get moving." Taylor crept away from Rosie.

"Are you sure you don't want to come along?" Rosie asked.

"No. Uh ..." Taylor said, "I have something else to do."

"All right." Rosie strolled up the path. "See you later," she called.

Rosie didn't worry about Taylor's strange actions. He always acted a little peculiar.

As Rosie climbed a hill, she heard more talking. This time she heard two voices. It sounded like Jill, the ground squirrel, and Toby, the cottontail rabbit.

Achoo! Rosie pulled a tissue out of her tennis shoe. She blew her nose. Then she hurried to the top of the hill. Where were her friends?

Rosie looked behind a big rock. She looked under a mesquite bush. Then she looked inside a log. She couldn't find Jill or Toby. Where were they? Why had they left so suddenly? Something was going on. And she had been left out!

Just then a loud flapping sound startled Rosie. She looked up to see Fergus, the owl, flying away. Strange! He was holding his nose. What was going on? First Taylor, then Jill and Toby, now Fergus. Why were they all acting so strangely around her?

Maybe Bert could explain this mystery. Rosie shuffled toward his bush house. The tips of two very long ears poked up from behind a rock next to the path. "Is that you, Jamal?" Rosie called.

"Rosie?" the jackrabbit asked. "What are you doing here?"

Rosie could only see his ears and his eyes as Jamal peeked over the rock. "I'm on my way to Bert's. Do you want to come help us find the best place for the clubhouse?"

"Well, I, well ..." Jamal mumbled.

"Why are you hiding?" Rosie shouted. "Come out!"

Jamal hopped out from behind the rock.

Ho! Ho! Hee! Rosie rolled over on her side from laughing so hard. A red bandana covered Jamal's nose.

"You look like a robber!" Rosie said.

"I'm not a robber!" Jamal said. "It's just that ... well ... Fergus said ..." Jamal paused.

"What did Fergus say that would make you wear your bandana over your nose?"

"Well ... he said that you stink." Jamal stared at his big feet.

"Fergus said I stink?" Rosie shouted.

"Yes," Jamal said. "Sorry, but I have to go now."

Rosie watched as the jackrabbit leaped over rocks. Why had Fergus said she stunk? Why had her friends believed him? She sniffed. She couldn't smell anything. Rosie cared about her friends. Now they were avoiding her because of some dumb tale. What was she going to do?

"Hey, Rosie!" The voice made her jump. Bert called her name again. "Rosie!"

"I'm right here," Rosie mumbled.

The roadrunner zoomed up to her. "Here you are!" he said. "I've been waiting for you. I'm ready to go exploring."

"You're always ready to go exploring!" Rosie said.

Bert laughed. "You're right. I am!" He took his pack off his back. Then he opened it. "See? I have a water bottle, my map, and a flashlight. Look! I even brought a measuring tape in case we need to measure anything."

"I'm sorry you had to wait, but I've had a strange morning."
Achoo!

"Oh?" The roadrunner paced
back and forth. Back and forth.
Back and forth.

Sniff. "First, Taylor kept backing away from me," Rosie reported. "Next, Jill and Toby disappeared before I could say hi to them."

"Really?" Bert scratched his head.

"Then Jamal was hiding behind a rock with his bandana covering his nose. He didn't even try to tell me a joke."

"Oh, dear," Bert said. "That is strange behavior for him!" He laughed.

"Fergus told him I stink!" Rosie sniffed. "Did Fergus tell you that too?"

"Most everyone loves to tell tales." The roadrunner put his pack on his back. *Grunt. Groan.* "I heard that same story from someone else."

"Do I stink?" Rosie asked.

"Not right now! You never have," Bert said. "But yesterday Fergus flew over a skunk that did."

"Now all my friends are afraid to be around me."

"I'm not," Bert said. "Don't worry about the rest of them. They'll figure out the whole truth."

Rosie sniffed.

"In the meantime," Bert said, "let's go find the best place for the clubhouse." *Zoom!* The road-runner took off. Rosie hurried after him. She followed Bert around rocks. She followed him around logs. She followed him around bushes. *Pant! Puff!*

25

Suddenly Bert put on his brakes. *Screech!* Rosie stopped too. Bert pulled his measuring tape out of his backpack.

"This looks like a great place for the clubhouse," Rosie said.

"Could be. Hold this, please." Bert handed Rosie the end of the

SCREEECH

measuring tape. Then he zoomed
around taking measurements
between the trees and the bushes.
He stopped to point. "The rabbits
could use that sand pile for their
hopping contests."

27

"Yes," Rosie said. "We could build the clubhouse right next to that cottonwood tree. That way the birds would have a place close by for their tree house." *Achoo!*

"This is a perfect place!" Bert poked the measuring tape down into his pack. "Let's go tell the others." He put his pack on his back.

"I had better not go with you." *Sniff!* "They don't like me anymore."

"You can't give up on your friends," Bert said. "We'll go to Wanda and Toby's burrow first. It's close by."

"Okay, but ..."

Zoom!

Rosie ran after Bert. She ran around bushes. She ran around logs. She ran around rocks. *Pant! Puff!*

Screech! Bert put on the brakes again. His tail stood straight up in the air.

Rosie stopped too.

"Did you hear that?" the roadrunner asked.

Grrrr! Rosie heard a growl.

"Sounds like a coyote!" Bert yelled. "Look! He's at Toby and Wanda's house." *Zoom!* Bert darted toward the coyote.

Rosie crept forward. Hiding under an acacia bush, she watched the coyote. He snooped and sniffed outside the cottontails' burrow.

The skunk watched as Bert darted toward the coyote. He pecked at the coyote's back feet. *Peck! Peck! Peck!*

The coyote jerked around. He swatted Bert with his paw. Bert tumbled to the ground.

Rosie ran out from under the bush. She had to help her friends. But what could she do? The coyote might eat her too!

Dust flew as the coyote dug at the burrow. Bert stood up. He shook himself off.

Shriek! Shriek! Rosie could hear the high-pitched cries of the cottontail rabbits. The coyote was getting close to Wanda and Toby. Bert raced toward the coyote. So did Rosie!

The coyote moved toward Bert.
The coyote stopped when he saw
the skunk. Rosie stopped too. She
shook. Was he going to eat her? Or
was he afraid to be around her too?

Then the coyote
began digging again.
Dig! Dig! Dig!

  Shriek! Shriek!

Bert flapped his wings. *Flap! Flap! Flap!* "Spray, Rosie, spray!" he shouted.

Suddenly Rosie stamped her feet. Then she spun around. After lifting her tail, Rosie sprayed the coyote. He howled. He snorted like a pig. *Snort! Snort! Snort!* He rubbed his eyes. Then he tucked his tail between his legs and ran away.

"*Yeah!*" Rosie's friends cheered. Jill and Lenny, the pack rat, scurried out of the bushes. Taylor toddled out of the bushes. Rosie saw Fergus up in a tree, watching it all. Wanda and Toby hopped out of their burrow. They looked both ways.

Achoo! Toby and Taylor sneezed. *Achoo!* Jill and Wanda sneezed. *Achoo!* Lenny sneezed.

Jamal leaped out from behind a rock. His bandana still covered his nose.

"*Hee! Hee! Ho!*" Taylor laughed. "*Ho! Ho! Ha!*" Lenny laughed. Then everybody laughed. Jamal pulled his bandana off his nose. *Cough! Cough!* Then he laughed too.

"You saved our lives, Rosie!" Wanda shouted. Toby nodded in agreement. Each of them gave her a big hug. *Squeeze! Squeeze!*

"But now I really *do* stink!" Rosie said. *Cough! Cough! Cough!*

"Yes, but your stink is what chased the coyote away," Bert said. He rubbed his beak. "God gave you that smelly spray so you can protect yourself and your friends. That's the only time you stink like that."

The owl flew over to a branch near Rosie. "I'm sorry, Rosie," Fergus said. "I was telling smelly tales, and I didn't tell the truth."

Rosie smiled at everyone. "I forgive you," she said. "Friends make mistakes. And friends forgive each other. And," she stopped to giggle, "they put up with a little stink now and then." All the desert critters giggled.

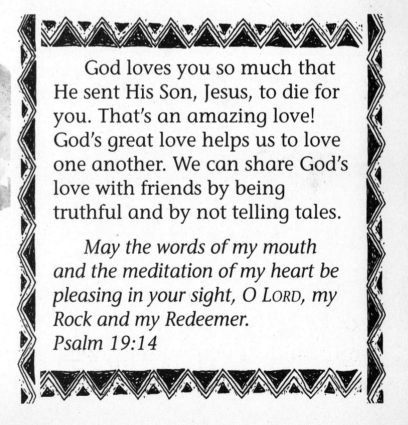

God loves you so much that He sent His Son, Jesus, to die for you. That's an amazing love! God's great love helps us to love one another. We can share God's love with friends by being truthful and by not telling tales.

May the words of my mouth and the meditation of my heart be pleasing in your sight, O LORD, my Rock and my Redeemer.
Psalm 19:14

Hi kids!

The next page has a message to you from God's Word. Use this code to find out what it is.

Code

A	D	E	F	G	I

K	L	M	N	O	P

R	S	T	U	V	Y	Z

Message

___ ___ ___ ___ ___ ___ ___ ___

___ ___ ___ ___ ___ ___

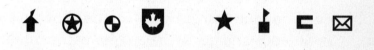
___ ___ ___ ___ ___ ___ ___ ___

___ ___ ___ ___ ___ ___ ___

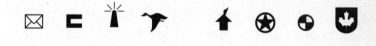
___ ___ ___ ___ ___ ___ ___ ___

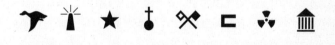
___ ___ ___ ___ ___ ___ ___ ___

___ ___ ___ ___ .

Psalm 34:13

45

For Parents and Teachers:

We've all fallen victim to smelly tales—probably more than once. No doubt this desert critter story evoked memories of instances when you were in Rosie's place, being shunned or misunderstood because of rumors and half-truths.

Being the brunt of someone else's joke or rumor is painful. Many people, especially children, might withdraw in an attempt to protect themselves from such situations. Bert didn't let Rosie do that. Instead he encouraged her to face her friends and get to the bottom of the rumor and expose the truth.

We are not always the victim in humiliating situations. It's likely that we've hurt others by spreading gossip. After smelling one skunk's spray, Fergus assumed every skunk would smell that badly. He lost no time in telling everyone what he thought.

Did Fergus make the assumption that all skunks sprayed and stunk for no particular reason? Or did he purposely leave out important details to create interest in his story? Whatever the case, he didn't give all the facts. Fergus' version of the story created apprehension in the desert critter friends, causing them to shun Rosie. Only Bert responded thoughtfully and befriended Rosie.

Help your children understand that God

helps us to show love to one another—to be kind to one another and to stand up for truth. Gossip, false tales, and half-truths only hurt.

Here are some questions and activities you can use as discussion starters to help your children understand these concepts.

Discussion Starters

1. Why did Taylor back away from Rosie? Why did Jamal hide from her?

2. Has anybody ever told tales about you? How did that make you feel? What did you do?

3. Why did Fergus say that Rosie stunk?

4. What was the truth about skunks and why they spray?

5. Have you ever spread tales about someone? Are you sorry? If you are sorry, ask God to forgive you. If you hurt someone's feelings, ask that person to forgive you too.

6. The next time you hear gossip about someone, how will you react? Like Taylor? Like Jill and Toby? Like Jamal? Or like Bert? Draw a picture of the animal you chose.

Pray together. Thank God for sending His Son to be your Savior. Ask God to forgive you for those times when you've gossiped or hurt someone's feelings because of something someone else said about that person. Ask God to help you be a good friend.

God will help you to be kind to others. Use these lines to tell me what you will do the next time someone tries to spread smelly tales.

_____

_____

_____

_____